Tom's Travels!

Written by Colleen Speight

and illustrated by Neil Wilkinson

Tom's Travels!
Copyright © Colleen Speight and Neil Wilkinson 2011

First published and distributed in 2011 by Gatehouse Media Limited

ISBN: 978-1-84231-079-3

British Library Cataloguing-in-Publication Data:
A catalogue record for this book is available from the British Library

This is Tom.

Tom is now in prison.

Tom wants to read.

Tom wants to read books.

Tom wants to read the paper.

Tom wants to read about football.

Tom wants to order his canteen.

He likes chocolate.

Tom has a friend called Dean.

Dean can read.

Dean is reading the Travellers' Times.

Tom wants to read the Travellers' Times.

Dean helps Tom read the Travellers' Times.

Dean and Tom read the Travellers' Times together.

Activity 1: Copy the words

Copy each sentence onto the line below.

This is Tom.

_____

Tom is now in prison.

_____

Tom wants to read.

_____

Tom wants to read books.

_____

Activity 2: Copy the words

Copy each sentence onto the line below.

Tom wants to read about football.

_____

Tom wants to order his canteen.

_____

He likes chocolate.

_____

Tom has a friend called Dean.

_____

Dean can read.

_____

Activity 3: Copy the words

Copy each sentence onto the line below.

Dean is reading the Travellers' Times.

_____

Tom wants to read The Travellers' Times.

_____

Dean helps Tom read the Travellers' Times.

_____

Dean and Tom read the Travellers' Times together.

_____

_____

Activity 4: Missing words

Choose the missing word from the box below to complete the sentence and add full stops.

1. This is _____

2. Tom is now in _____

3. Tom wants to _____

4. Tom wants to read _____

5. Tom wants to read the _____

6. Tom wants to read about _____

7. Tom wants to order his _____

8. He likes _____

chocolate	football	prison
	canteen	Tom
read	paper	books

Activity 5: Missing words

Choose the missing word from the box below to complete the sentence. You may use a word more than once. Remember to add full stops.

1. Tom has a friend called _____

2. Dean can _____

3. Dean is reading the _____

4. Tom wants to _____ the _____ Times.

5. Dean helps Tom read the Travellers' _____

6. Dean and _____ read the _____ Times _____

together	Dean	read
Tom	Travellers'	Times

Activity 6: All about Tom

Circle the correct answer.

1. **Tom wants to**

   sleep / chat / read

2. **Tom wants to read about**

   tennis / cricket / football

3. **Tom wants to order his**

   trainers / canteen / radio

4. **Tom likes**

   apples / chocolate / crisps

5. **Tom has a friend called**

   Dean / Darren / Danny

6. **Tom wants to read**

   books / leaflets / magazines

7. **Which book or paper do you like to read?**

   _____

Activity 7: Tom is in a muddle

Put the words in the correct order to make a sentence. Add capital letters and full stops.

1. this tom is

_____

2. is now in tom prison

_____

3. read wants to tom

_____

4. books read wants to tom

_____

5. the paper read wants to tom

_____

6. football to read tom about wants

_____

7. to order wants canteen tom his

_____

Activity 8: Tom is still mixed up!

Put the words in the correct order to make a sentence.
Add capital letters and full stops.

1. chocolate likes he

   _____

2. dean called a friend tom has

   _____

3. can read dean

   _____

4. travellers' is dean the reading times

   _____

5. wants tom the times read to travellers'

   _____

6. tom dean read helps travellers' times the

   _____

7. and tom dean times read the together travellers'

_____

_____

Gatehouse Books®

Gatehouse Books are written for older teenagers and adults who are developing their basic reading and writing or English language skills.

The format of our books is clear and uncluttered.
The language is familiar and the text is often line-broken, so that each line ends at a natural pause.

Gatehouse Books are widely used within Adult Basic Education throughout the English speaking world. They are also a valuable resource within the Prison Education Service and Probation Services, Social Services and secondary schools - both in basic skills and ESOL teaching situations.

Catalogue available

Gatehouse Media Limited
PO Box 965
Warrington
WA4 9DE

Tel/Fax: 01925 267778
E-mail: info@gatehousebooks.com
Website: www.gatehousebooks.com